THE SOURCES OF THE STORIES

There are many versions of the fairy tales told
in this book. The storytellers listed below
wrote, or wrote down, the best-known versions,
on which the present tellings are based. The
date is the original year of publication.

Snow White and the Seven Dwarfs · Jacob and Wilhelm Grimm 1812
The Old Woman in Luck · Flora Annie Steel 1918
The Three Billy Goats Gruff · P.C. Asbjörnsen and J.I. Moe 1843

Copyright © 1985 by Walker Books Ltd.
All rights reserved.
This 1986 edition is published by Derrydale Books, distributed by
Crown Publishers, Inc., 225 Park Avenue South, New York,
New York 10003, by arrangement with Walker Books, Ltd.
Manufactured in Italy
Library of Congress Cataloging in Publication Data
Hayes, Sarah.
Snow White and the seven dwarfs ; The old woman in luck ;
The three Billy goats gruff.
(Read me a story)
Summary: A simple retelling of three traditional tales from
German, English, and Norwegian sources.
1. Fairy tales. [1. Fairy tales. 2. Folklore]
I. Anstey, Caroline, ill. II. Absjørnsen, Peter Christen, 1812–1885.
Tre bukkene Bruse. III. Steel, Flora Annie Webster, 1847–1929.
Old woman in luck.
IV. Schneewittchen. V. Title. VI. Series: Hayes, Sarah.
Read me a story.
PZ8.H314873Sn 1986 398.2′1′   86-11623
ISBN 0-517-61556-8
h g f e d c b a

SNOW WHITE
AND THE
SEVEN DWARFS

THE OLD WOMAN IN LUCK

THE THREE BILLY GOATS GRUFF

Retold by Sarah Hayes

Illustrated by Caroline Anstey

DERRYDALE BOOKS • NEW YORK

SNOW WHITE
AND THE SEVEN DWARFS

Once upon a time a young queen sat by a window sewing. As she gazed at the snowflakes falling, her needle slipped and pricked her finger. A drop of blood welled up. 'Alas,' she sighed, 'how I wish I could bear a child as white as snow, as red as blood and as black as the ebony of the window frame.'

A year later the young queen's wish was granted, and she gave birth to a daughter with skin as white as snow, lips as red as blood and hair as black as ebony. 'Let her be called Snow White,' were the queen's last words, for she died soon after the baby was born.

When Snow White was a year old, the king married again. His new queen was beautiful,

but she was proud and jealous
and full of wicked schemes.
She had a secret room in the
castle where a magic mirror
hung, and there she would
stand, gazing at her
reflection and saying:

'Mirror, mirror, on the wall,
Who is the fairest one of all?'

The mirror would answer:

'You, O Queen,
are the fairest one.'

And the queen would
smile and be satisfied.

Yet every day little Snow White grew more beautiful, and the wicked queen more jealous. On the day of Snow White's tenth birthday, the queen once again slipped off to her secret room and stood before her magic glass.

'Mirror, mirror, on the wall,
Who is the fairest one of all?'

The mirror always spoke the truth.

'You, O Queen, have beauty rare,
But Snow White is ten times more fair.'

The queen raged and fumed, hating Snow White. She called a huntsman and told him to take Snow White into the forest and kill her. 'Bring me her heart so I may know she is dead,' said the wicked queen.

Snow White was very frightened when the huntsman took her deep into the forest and drew his knife. She looked up into his face and tears rolled down her cheeks. The huntsman took mercy on her and told her to run off into the forest. On his way home he killed a young deer and cut out its heart to give to the queen.

The forest was dark and dangerous and full of wild beasts. Snow White ran and ran until she came to a clearing where a little cottage stood. Desperate for food and rest, she pushed open the door and entered. No one was at home, but a meal had been laid for seven people on a low table covered with a white cloth. Snow White took a taste from each of the seven bowls, hoping the owners would not notice, and took a sip from each of the seven cups. Then she tried each of the neat little beds in the bedroom. Some were too small, some were too narrow or too high, but one was perfect. Snow White soon fell fast asleep.

She did not hear the tramp, tramp of seven pairs of boots, nor the crash of seven pickaxes being thrown on the floor. The cottage belonged to seven dwarfs who spent their days mining for silver and gold in the hills beyond the forest.

'Now who's been sitting in my chair?' asked one.

'Who's been scraping my bowl?' asked another.

'Who's been supping with my spoon?' asked a third.

'And who is this, lying in my bed?' asked the seventh.

'Who's been cutting with my knife?' asked a fourth.

'Who's been eating my bread?' asked a fifth.

'Who's been drinking from my cup?' asked a sixth.

The dwarfs ran to look and were so taken with Snow White's beauty that they did not want to wake her. That night the seventh dwarf shared a bed with the others, an hour with each.

When she awoke, Snow White was alarmed by the sight of the seven little men clustered around her, but they made her so welcome that she was soon quite at home. The dwarfs were shocked at her story and made Snow White promise to stay with them.

'You can cook and clean and keep house for us,' said one.

'We shall be away all day, though,' said another.

'You must take great care,' said a third.

'The wicked queen is sure to come and look for you,' said a fourth.

'Let no one in,' said a fifth.

'No one,' echoed the sixth and seventh.

So Snow White kept house for the seven dwarfs, and a very merry house it was for a month or two. Then one day the wicked queen went to her secret room and looked into her magic glass.

'Mirror, mirror, on the wall,
Who is the fairest one of all?'

The mirror answered:

'You, O Queen, have beauty rare,
Yet lives there one ten times more fair.
In seven dwarfs' house by yonder hill,
Snow White is the fairer still.'

The queen fumed and raged and plotted all night how she might kill Snow White. In the morning she painted her face and disguised herself as an old peddlar. Carrying a basket piled high with ribbons and lace and trimmings of all colors, she made her way to the seven dwarfs' cottage.

'Ribbons and laces for sale,' she called. 'Pretty ribbons.'

Snow White looked out of the window and saw the bright colors of the peddlar's basket. She opened the door and chose a ribbon.

'Let me lace you up,' said the old woman. 'You can be laced properly for once.' Snow White suspected nothing, and she stood quietly while the woman threaded the ribbon through once, twice, three, four times. Then she pulled the laces so tightly that Snow White could not breathe, and she fell to the floor.

'Now we shall see who is the fairest one of all,' said the queen, and she hurried away.

When the seven dwarfs returned and found their dear Snow White on the ground, they were horrified. Four of them lifted her up and three cut the laces that were suffocating her. In a moment or two Snow White recovered.

'That was no peddlar,' said one of the dwarfs.

'That was the wicked queen,' said another.

'You must promise to let no one in while we are away,' said a third sternly.

'I promise,' Snow White said.

The queen meanwhile went into her secret room and stood before the magic mirror.

'Mirror, mirror, on the wall,
Who is the fairest one of all?'

The mirror answered:

'You, O Queen, have beauty rare,
Yet lives there one ten times more fair.
In seven dwarfs' house by yonder hill,
Snow White is the fairer still.'

The queen's face grew pale with fury. Snow White was alive! All night she fumed and raged and plotted, and by morning she had made a jeweled comb so poisonous it would kill anyone who used it. Disguised as a gypsy, she made her way to the dwarfs' cottage.

'Bracelets and bows,' she called. 'Trinkets and combs.'

Snow White looked out of the window. 'I dare not let you in,' she said, but the gypsy held up the comb and let the light catch the jewels. Snow White ran to open the door.

'Let me comb your hair,' said the gypsy. 'It is so long and beautiful.' As soon as the comb touched her hair, the poison took effect and Snow White fell to the ground.

'So much for your beauty,' said the wicked queen and hurried back to the castle.

When the dwarfs came home, they quickly pulled out the poisoned comb and Snow White revived. This time they made Snow White swear to let no one in.

At the castle the queen stood once more before her magic mirror.

'Mirror, mirror, on the wall,
Who is the fairest one of all?'

The mirror answered:

'You, O Queen, have beauty rare,
Yet lives there one ten times more fair.
In seven dwarfs' house by yonder hill,
Snow White is the fairer still.'

The queen shrieked with fury. She ground her teeth with rage. All night long she fumed and muttered and schemed. With the aid of her black arts she made a poisoned apple, one half green, the other half rosy red, and laid it on top of a basket of apples. Then she disguised herself as an old apple woman and made her way to the dwarfs' cottage.

'Apples, red rosy apples,' she called.

'I dare not come down,' said Snow White, looking out of the window.

'Take an apple then,' said the old woman, throwing her the poisoned apple.

'I dare not,' said Snow White, throwing it back.

'Afraid of poison, eh?' said the old woman, and cut the apple in two. 'Look, I will eat one half, and you can eat the other.'

Now the apple had been so cleverly contrived that only one half was poisoned. The old woman bit into the green half, and Snow White stretched out her hand to take the rosy red half. She had hardly taken one bite before the poison began to work and she fell lifeless to the ground.

'Black as ebony, red as blood and white as death,' said the wicked queen and hurried back to the castle to look into her magic mirror.

'Mirror, mirror, on the wall,
Who is the fairest one of all?'

The mirror answered:

'You, O Queen, are the fairest one.'

The queen was satisfied, for she knew that Snow White was dead at last.

When the dwarfs returned and found Snow White, they did everything they could think of to revive her. They cut her laces, loosened her dress, combed her hair, lifted her up, poured water over her, but all was in vain. Snow White lay dead. The dwarfs lamented loud and long, for they had loved Snow White. She was so beautiful, even in death, that the dwarfs could not bear to bury her in the ground.

Instead they laid her in a coffin of clear glass
with a gold inscription around it that told her
name and said she was a king's daughter.
They carried it to a high mountain and
took turns keeping watch by it.

Five years passed, and then a king's son
lost his way in the forest and had to spend the
night in the dwarfs' house. He saw the glass
coffin high on the mountain and was struck
with Snow White's beauty, undimmed by the
years that had passed. He could not bear to

leave Snow White and pressed the dwarfs to give him the coffin. At first they refused, but he was so earnest that at last they agreed.

As he rode along, gazing at Snow White's face, one of the servants carrying the coffin stumbled and the piece of poisoned apple was dislodged from Snow White's throat. She opened her eyes and saw the king's son. 'Where am I?' she asked.

'You are with me,' said the king's son and lifted her onto his horse.

Snow White and her prince were soon married, and invitations were sent out for a grand banquet. The wicked queen put on her finest gown for the wedding feast, and smiled triumphantly at her reflection in the glass.

'Mirror, mirror, on the wall,
Who is the fairest one of all?'

The mirror answered:

'You, O Queen, have beauty rare,
But the king's son's queen is ten
times more fair.'

The wicked queen stormed off to the wedding. When she saw that the bride was none other than Snow White, she was transfixed with fury, unable to move. Two iron shoes were heated till they were red-hot, and the wicked queen was made to put them on and dance and dance till she dropped down dead.

THE OLD WOMAN IN LUCK

One day a poor lonely old woman was
walking home when she found a large
black cooking pot in a ditch. 'I am in luck!'
she exclaimed. 'I expect there's a hole in that
pot, but I can still use it for planting flowers.'

She picked up the pot and
wrapped it in her shawl. The road
was long and the pot was heavy, so
the old woman soon stopped for a
rest. She sat down and unwrapped
the shawl to take another look at
the pot. To her surprise it was full
to the top with shiny gold pieces.

'I am in luck!' she exclaimed.
'All those gold pieces for a poor
old woman like me.'

She wrapped up the pot and went on her way, but soon she sat down to rest again. She untied the shawl to take another look at her treasure, but she found to her surprise that the pot of gold had turned into a lump of silver.

'I am in luck!' she exclaimed. 'All those gold pieces would have been such a trouble to me, always getting lost or stolen.'

She tied up the lump of silver and went on her way, but soon she was ready to rest again. She sat down to undo the shawl. To her amazement the silver had turned into a lump of iron.

'I am in luck!' she exclaimed. 'What does an old woman want with silver and gold to keep her awake at night worrying about burglars? Iron now I can sell for pennies. And pennies are what an old woman needs.'

She tied up the bundle and went on her way. Soon she could see the gate of her cottage at the bottom of the hill. She sat down for a last rest and untied the bundle for a last peep. The lump of iron had turned into a large stone.

'I am in luck!' she exclaimed. 'This stone is just what I need to keep my gate from slamming.'

She tied up the stone and walked down the hill to the cottage. When she reached her front gate, she sat down to undo the shawl and get out the stone. But as she untied the knot, the bundle began to swell. A long pointed ear poked out of one corner, then a snout appeared, and another ear, then four long lanky legs and a floppy tail. The shawl fell to the ground, and there, squealing and whinnying and as big as a haystack, stood a bogle-beast. The old woman watched as the bogle-beast danced around her three times and then capered off over the hill.

'I am in luck!' exclaimed the old woman. 'Fancy seeing a bogle-beast, and me only a poor lonely old woman. I must be the luckiest poor lonely old woman in the whole wide world.' And she went to bed as cheerful as ever.

The strange thing is that from that day onward the old woman's luck changed and she was never poor or lonely again.

THE THREE
BILLY GOATS GRUFF

Once upon a time there were three billy goats who went by the name of Gruff. They had fine pastures to graze, but they longed to reach the meadow of sweet grass which lay on the other side of the river. In order to get there they had to go over a bridge. Under the bridge lived a wicked troll with staring eyes and a long nose.

The youngest billy goat Gruff stepped onto the bridge. *'Trip trap, trip trap,'* went his hooves. Out popped the troll.

'Who's that trip-trapping over my bridge?' he roared.

'It is only I, the youngest billy goat Gruff, going across to the sweet grass meadow,' said the youngest billy goat Gruff in a tiny voice.

'I'm going to eat you up!' roared the troll.

'Oh, please don't do that. My brother is coming behind me, and he is much bigger than I am,' said the youngest billy goat Gruff.

'Be off with you then,' said the troll, and the youngest billy goat Gruff trip-trapped over the bridge and into the sweet grass meadow.

After a while the second billy goat Gruff stepped onto the bridge. 'TRIP TRAP, TRIP TRAP, TRIP TRAP,' went his hooves. Out popped the troll.

'Who's that trip-trapping over my bridge?' he roared.

'It is only I, the second billy goat Gruff, going across to the sweet grass meadow,' said the second billy goat Gruff in a middling sort of voice.

'I'm going to eat you up!' roared the troll.

'Oh, please don't do that. My brother is coming behind me, and he is much bigger than I am,' said the second billy goat Gruff.

'Be off with you then,' said the troll, and the second billy goat Gruff trip-trapped over the bridge and into the sweet grass meadow.

Just then the great big billy goat Gruff stepped onto the bridge. 'TRIP TRAP, TRIP TRAP, TRIP TRAP,' went his hooves very loudly. Out popped the troll.

'Who's that tramping TRIP TRAP, TRIP TRAP over my bridge?' he roared.

'It is only I, great big billy goat Gruff, going across to the sweet grass meadow,' said the great big billy goat Gruff in a deep voice.

'I'm going to eat you up!' roared the troll.

But the great big billy goat Gruff bellowed:

'Come on then, show you have no fears.
I've four great stones and two sharp spears.'

The troll climbed onto the bridge. The biggest billy goat Gruff lowered his head and flew at the troll, his horns like spears and his hooves clattering like stones. He butted the troll over the bridge and into the river, where he was swept away and never seen again.

As for the billy goats Gruff, they lived happily in the meadow of sweet grass and all three became very fat.